629.13 Jaffe, Elizabeth D.
JAF   Pilots

SOUTH RUTLAND
ELEMENTARY LIBRARY

Pilots
Community Workers

by Elizabeth Dana Jaffe

Content Adviser: Captain John Feldvary,
Air Line Pilots Association, International

Reading Adviser: Dr. Linda D. Labbo,
College of Education, Department of Reading Education,
The University of Georgia

COMPASS POINT BOOKS

Minneapolis, Minnesota

Many thanks to Randy, the pilot

To Gwen and Tony, who could not be more loved

Compass Point Books
3722 West 50th Street, #115
Minneapolis, MN 55410

Visit Compass Point Books on the Internet at *www.compasspointbooks.com* or e-mail your request to *custserv@compasspointbooks.com*

Photographs ©: David Frazier, cover; William B. Folsom, 4, 20, 24; Gustav W. Verderber/Visuals Unlimited, 5; Peter Holden/Visuals Unlimited, 6; Jeff Greenbergy/Visuals Unlimited, 7, 14; Photo Network/Jeff Greenberg, 8; Photo Network/David Vinyard, 9; Kelly-Mooney Photography/Corbis, 10; Unicorn Stock Photos/Jean Higgins, 11; Sean McCoy, 12; Mark E. Gibson/Visuals Unlimited, 13; A. J. Copley/Visuals Unlimited, 15; Photo Network/Mary Messenger, 16; Unicorn Stock Photos/Jeff Greenberg, 17; Photo Network/Douglas Pulsipher; James L. Shaffer, 19; Tom J. Ulrich/Visuals Unlimited, 22; Beth Davidow/Visuals Unlimited, 23; Unicorn Stock Photos/Dennis Thompson, 25; Photri-Microstock, 26; Unicorn Stock Photos/Florent Flipper, 27.

Editors: E. Russell Primm and Emily J. Dolbear
Photo Researcher: Svetlana Zhurkina
Photo Selector: Linda S. Koutris
Designer: Bradfordesign, Inc.

Library of Congress Cataloging-in-Publication Data

Jaffe, Elizabeth D.
    Pilots / by Elizabeth D. Jaffe.
      p. cm. — (Community workers)
    Includes bibliographical references and index.
    Summary: Introduces the work of commercial airplane and jet pilots, including duties, training, skills needed, and contribution to the community.
    ISBN 0-7565-0065-6
     1. Aeronautics—Vocational guidance—Juvenile literature. 2. Airplanes—Piloting—Vocational guidance—Juvenile literature. 3. Air pilots —Juvenile literature. [1. Air pilots. 2. Airplanes—Piloting. 3. Occupations.] I. Title. II. Series.
    TL561 .J34 2001
    629.13'023—dc   2100-011500

© 2001 by Compass Point Books
All rights reserved. No part of this book may be reproduced without written permission from the publisher. The publisher takes no responsibility for the use of any of the materials or methods described in this book, nor for the products thereof.
Printed in the United States of America.

Table of Contents

What Do Pilots Do?	5
What Tools and Equipment Do They Use?	7
How Do Pilots Help?	9
Where Do They Work?	11
Who Do They Work With?	13
What Do They Wear?	17
What Training Does It Take?	19
What Skills Do They Need?	21
What Problems Do They Face?	23
Would You Like to Be a Pilot?	25
A Pilot's Tools and Clothes	26
In the Cockpit	27
A Pilot's Day	28
Glossary	29
Did You Know?	30
Want to Know More?	31
Index	32

What Do Pilots Do?

Pilots fly **aircraft**. Some pilots carry people from place to place in airplanes. They make sure the people in the plane are safe. Some pilots spray crops. Some pilots put out forest fires. Some pilots work for the air force.

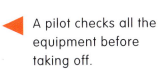

A pilot checks all the equipment before taking off.

A military pilot

What Tools and Equipment Do They Use?

Pilots use airplane controls to check the plane's fuel and speed. They use a radio and headphones to talk to people in the control tower on the ground.

Pilots also use a tool that helps fly the plane for them. This tool is called the **autopilot**. Pilots never use the autopilot during takeoffs or landings though.

Headphones help pilots stay in touch with people on the ground.

A pilot checks the airplane controls.

How Do Pilots Help?

Pilots take people, products, and mail from place to place. Some pilots spray crops to keep them free of pests. Some pilots keep forest fires from spreading. Military pilots help protect their country.

◀ Pilots help people— young and old— travel all over the world.

Pilots who fly military planes help keep people in their country safe. ▶

Where Do They Work?

Pilots work in airports. They meet with their **crew** in the crew room before takeoff. Then they work in a **cockpit** on the airplane. The cockpit is a small room at the front of the plane with the controls. Pilots fly many miles in the sky to places around the world.

The inside of a cockpit

A pilot checks the outside of the plane before takeoff.

Who Do They Work With?

The head pilot, or **captain**, often works with a copilot. The copilot is called a **first officer**. Pilots also work with people in control towers. They are called **air traffic controllers**. They tell the pilot when to take off and when to land. Pilots also work with **flight attendants.** These workers take care of the people on the airplane.

◀ Flight attendants are an important part of the flight crew.

Air traffic controllers help pilots fly safely. ▶

Pilots also work with a **ground crew**. Ground crews fix and clean airplanes. They fill the plane's tank with fuel. The crews also get all the bags and boxes on and off the aircraft.

◀ The ground crew loads bags and boxes onto the airplanes.

Workers pump fuel into an airplane before takeoff. ▶

What Do They Wear?

Pilots who work for airlines often wear a company uniform. The company usually gives them the same kind of suit and hat. The captain's uniform has more stripes than the first officer's uniform. That makes it easy to tell who is in charge on the airplane.

◀ A pilot in uniform

Military pilots wear a special uniform. ▶

What Training Does It Take?

Pilots study at a flying school or in the military. Pilots must take math and science classes. Then they learn how an aircraft works. They take lessons with flying teachers. Every pilot must pass written and flying tests.

Almost anyone can learn how to fly.

A flying student practices flying on a machine.

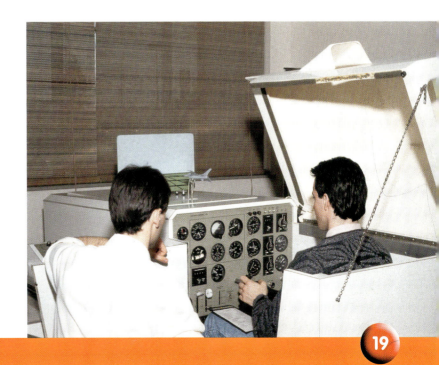

What Skills Do They Need?

Pilots have to give and take orders well. They must be able to talk to their crew and listen carefully. Pilots must always be alert. If something goes wrong, they have to think fast. Pilots also must have perfect vision—with or without glasses—and good hearing.

◄ Pilots must be prepared to fly when needed.

A pilot sprays chemicals from the sky to help put out fires. ▶

What Problems Do They Face?

Pilots spend many days away from home on long flights. They often fly at night. Pilots fly on weekends and holidays too. Sometimes they have to fly in bad weather. Sometimes their equipment breaks down. Pilots' jobs can be stressful but they must always stay calm. After all, pilots have to keep everyone on the plane safe.

◀ Flying military jets can be dangerous.

Pilots must make sure that their planes are always ready for takeoff. ▶

Would You Like to Be a Pilot?

Do you feel that flying is exciting? Do you like the idea of being in control of an airplane? Do you like to travel? Becoming a pilot is hard work. But it is a job that offers great adventure.

◀ Flying a large jet filled with hundreds of people is an important job.

Military pilots are very valuable to their country. ▶

A Pilot's Tools and Clothes

In the Cockpit

A Pilot's Day

Early morning
- A pilot arrives at the airport and checks the weather.
- The pilot asks the ground crew if the plane is ready for takeoff.
- Then in the cockpit, the pilot makes sure that the plane is ready.
- The pilot plans the flight with the first officer.

Noon
- The pilot asks the control tower if it is time to take off.
- The first officer checks the outside of the plane.
- The pilot steers the airplane down the runway, picks up speed, and takes off.
- When the plane is 10,000 feet (3,050 meters) in the air, the pilot turns on the autopilot.

Afternoon
- The pilot tells the flight crew what time the plane will land.

Evening
- As the airplane nears the airport, the pilot talks to the control tower about landing.
- The air traffic controller tells the pilot when and where to land.
- The pilot lands the plane smoothly.

Night
- After finishing some paperwork, the pilot heads to a hotel to sleep.

Glossary

aircraft—any machine that flies in the air

air traffic controllers—people in the control tower who tell the pilots when to take off and when to land

autopilot—a tool that helps pilots by flying the plane

captain—a person who tells the crew what to do and keeps the people on the plane safe

cockpit—the small room at the front of the plane with the controls

crew—a group of people who work together

first officer—copilot

flight attendants—workers who take care of the people on the plane

ground crew—workers who take care of the plane at the airport

Did You Know?

- The captain always sits on the left side of the cockpit. The first officer sits on the right side.

- The longer the flight, the higher pilots fly in the sky. The shorter the flight, the lower they fly in the sky.

- The captain is the only person who handles an airplane during takeoff and landing.

- When pilots can't see in bad weather, they use flight equipment to guide them to a safe landing.

Want to Know More?

At the Library
Flanagan, Alice K., and Romie Flanagan (photographer). *Flying an Agricultural Plane with Mr. Miller*. Danbury, Conn.: Children's Press, 1999.
Jefferis, David. *Flight: Fliers and Flying Machines*. New York: Franklin Watts, 1991.
Langley, Andrew. *Amelia Earhart: The Pioneering Pilot*. New York: Oxford University Press Children's Books, 1998.
Schomp, Virginia. *If You Were a Pilot*. Boston, Mass.: Benchmark Books, 2000.

On the Web
Air & Space Smithsonian Magazine
http://www.airspacemag.com/
For articles and pictures about all kinds of flying

Federal Aviation Association (FAA) Aviation Education
http://www.faa.gov/education/resource/kidcornr.htm
For word puzzles and experiments related to flying

Through the Mail
Federal Aviation Association (FAA)
800 Independence Avenue, S.W.
Washington, DC 20591
To get pamphlets and educational guides about flying

On the Road
Wright Brothers National Memorial
800 Colington Road
Kill Devil Hills, NC 27948
252/441-7430
To visit the site of the Wright brothers' first flights in 1903

Index

air force, 5, *5*, 9, *9*, 17, 22, 25, 26
air traffic controllers, 13, *13*, 28
aircraft, 5, *9*, *11*, *18*, *21*, *22*, *23*, 24
autopilot control, 7, 28
captains, 13, *27*
cockpit, *4*, *7*, *10*, 11, *27*
control tower, 13, 28
controls, *4*, 7, *7*, *10*, 27
copilots. *See* first officers.
crew. *See* flight crew; ground crew.

equipment, *26*
first officers, 13, *16*, *27*, 28
flight attendants, *12*, 13
flight crew, 11, *12*, 13, 21, 28
flight engineers, 27
flying school, *18*, 19, *19*
fuel, 15, *15*
ground crew, *14*, 15, *15*, 21, *24*, 28
headphones, *6*
pilots, *4*, *6*, *7*, *11*, *16*, *18*, *20*, *23*, *26*
uniforms, *16*, 17, *17*, *26*
weather, 23, 28

About the Author
After graduating from Brown University, Elizabeth Dana Jaffe received her master's degree in early education from and taught at Bank Street College of Education in New York City. Since then, she has written and edited educational materials. Her books include *Can You Eat a Fraction?* and *Sojourner Truth*. Elizabeth Dana Jaffe lives in New York City.

SOUTH RUTLAND
ELEMENTARY LIBRARY